Check

by Nia Kweli

Cover and interior illustrations by Nia Kweli
ISBN: 979-8-9942003-0-8
Printed in the United States of America

For more information, visit: www.truthbusters.info.

For my children – Marquis and McKenzie
May you always see what others miss,
and know that your voice is never small.

"The most powerful truths are often not hidden by darkness, but by light so bright we forget to question it."
Nia Kweli

Contents

Opening Moves

The Board breathed.
It always did quietly, patiently the way ancient things do.

Sixty-four squares. Thirty-two pieces.
Half White. Half Black.
A kingdom divided not by walls, but by design.

Each morning, a mist would rise from the center squares,
where the light wavered, and no side truly ruled.
And on either end, two great Houses stirred to life
divided not just by distance, but by rhythm, by memory,
by the oldest rule of the game:
White moves first. Black must respond.

To the South, on the warm and sun-drenched Black Squares, stood the **Onyx Keep**.
The air buzzed with cicadas and the scent of sweet earth.
Golden light poured through carved archways.
Trees bowed heavy with fruit.
Rain arrived in song, and the heat left nothing frozen.
The people here moved with ease, with rhythm, with memory guiding every step.

Each piece played its part:
• **Queen Zahara**, watchful and wise, robed in cloths dyed from earth and ink and history.
• **King Jabari**, carved of stillness and strength, keeper of the ancient board of stories.
• **Rook Kofi**, Zahara's brother, who walked the battlements reciting names of the forgotten.
• **Bishop Sade**, voice like thunder wrapped in silk.
• **Knight Luma**, niece of the Queen, whose eyes leapt ahead of every move.
• **Knight Tariq**, who moved through the borderlands like shadow.
And the **Pawns** young, agile, and many.

Nia, the youngest, never on time.
But always listening.

To the North, across the stiff center line, the **Ivory Hall** rose from frostbit-

ten ground.
The wind cut like sharpened bone.
Snow lay like silence across every roof.
Trees stood bare. The rivers slow and icy.
Colorless light pressed through clouded windows, dimming every morning.

Inside, the White Family polished their order:
- **King Alaric**, master of statutes and stone-faced silences.
- **Queen Isolde**, lips always curved with careful calculation.
- **Rook Blanche**, strict as a drawn sword.
- **Bishop Lucien**, hollow-eyed, reciting doctrine by rote.
- **Knight Elara**, the youngest adult, with questions she had been taught to bury.
- **Knight Gideon**, loyal, quiet, precise.

The Pawns in Ivory Hall rarely laughed.
Most had forgotten how.

For a long time, the two families lived in careful balance.
Children sometimes met on the middle line to toss stones or swap tunes.

Nia had once carved a lion from driftwood for a boy named **Silas**, a White Pawn.
He brought her a pressed flower, frozen in glass.
She smiled. He didn't.
But he didn't forget, either.

Even the Queens once shared a quiet tea in the garden between their Keeps.
Zahara brought honeyroot and heat.
Isolde brought sugar cubes dry and clinking in crystal.

They spoke of peace.
Of order.
Of beauty.

But the Board knew what the pieces did not.
That even a quiet game holds tension.
That sometimes the whole army shifts
just for a single check.

10

The weather had already whispered the deeper truth:

One side grows beneath sunlight.
The other, beneath frost.

And though no line had yet been crossed...
The first move had been made.

The Quiet Before

The wind at center square carried both heat and chill,
depending on which direction it came from.

Twilight draped the Board in hues neither side could fully claim.
Too golden for frost, too pale for fire.
The boundary stones glimmered where the light struck just right,
and in the soft hush of evening, most pieces retreated
to their respective corners.

But not all.

In a grove of silent, leafless trees just beyond the Eye of the Board
where, years ago, songs were exchanged in secret
and messages tucked into bark
two figures stood still, cloaked in shadow.

Knight Luma arrived first,
leaning slightly on her lance, though her stance betrayed no fatigue.
Her eyes scanned the familiar stone paths
not for threats, but for openings.
She was always watching.
Always thinking six moves ahead.

Knight Elara approached moments later,
her white cloak trimmed in ash gray.
She moved carefully,
as if the ground itself might report her presence.

They met without greeting.
They had done this before.
Always brief.
Always hidden.
But something had shifted.

"You shouldn't be here," Luma said, not turning.

"I know," Elara replied, glancing toward the northern mist.
"But I needed to ask… is it true?
The message your Bishop sent to ours
about the river trades being blocked?
That the Keep's supply lines are being watched?"

Luma tilted her head.

"We're watched everywhere.
Even in our own halls.
You're just now noticing?"

Elara's lips pressed tight.
"I've noticed.
I've just never said it out loud."

A silence stretched between them.
Not hostile.
But wary.
Like two Knights circling a contested square,
each waiting for the other to blink.

"They say in Ivory Hall," Elara murmured,
"that your Queen is hoarding resources.
That she's building armies.
Preparing for aggression."

"And in Onyx Keep," Luma replied,
"they say your King is rewriting the accords.
That your Rooks are redrawing maps
while your Bishops pray over war scrolls."

"Then we're both hearing lies," Elara said.

"Or truths, buried like traps under polished moves," Luma countered.

Their eyes met.
Not in trust.
But in recognition.
Not all pieces move straight.
Some bend. Some leap.
And some… switch sides when no one is looking.

"I don't want this to end in blood," Elara said.

Luma studied her.
"Do you believe you can stop it?"

Elara didn't answer right away.
A rook called from the tower behind her
a reminder of where she belonged.

"I don't know," she admitted.
"But I want to try."

Luma nodded slowly.
"Then move carefully, Knight.
Not all pieces wait for orders anymore."

Elara stepped back,
her cloak catching the last of the light.
"Then I'll move differently."

As she disappeared into the fading frost,
Luma turned back toward the warmth of the Keep.

The Board was stirring again.
And even silent pieces
were beginning to shift.

SMALL GAMES,
QUIET MOVES

In the soft light of early dusk,
the center of the Board glowed with a hazy warmth
that strange stretch of mist and silence
where neither Keep held dominion.

It was a quiet square.
One the Masters rarely mentioned.
Where the rules softened,
and no piece knew quite how to move.

Nia crouched near the edge of the Black Square side,
clutching a small pouch of carved stones.
Each one etched with a symbol: memory games
her aunt, Bishop Sade, had taught her as a child
a language of patterns, echoes, and instinct.

Across from her, on a frosted log just over the invisible line,
Silas sat stiffly with a book balanced on his knees.
He hadn't turned a page in five minutes.

They had met here a handful of times now
always by chance.
Always pretending it wasn't.

"You didn't bring your puzzle box," Nia said,
pretending not to care.

"I wasn't supposed to leave the Hall today," Silas muttered,
his eyes flicking toward the white banners
barely visible in the distance.
"But I told the Guard I was collecting frostweed samples."

Nia smirked. "You always have a good lie."

"I don't lie," he replied. "I rearrange facts."

"Same thing," she grinned,
tossing him a stone marked with the spiral.
"Your move."

Silas caught it, hesitated,

then placed it between them off-center.

"Do you ever wonder," he asked quietly,
"what it would be like if there was no line?"

Nia paused. Her fingers hovered over the next stone.

"No line?" she echoed.

"Yeah. No Black Squares. No White Squares.
Just… the Board. All of it."

She looked up, studying him.

"Would your King allow that?"

Silas lowered his gaze. "I'm just a Pawn."

"That's what they think," Nia said.
"But Pawns can cross the board.
They can choose who they become."

Silas gave a small, tired smile. "If they survive the middle."

A silence stretched between them.
Not tense just careful.
The kind of silence found between moves
when the outcome hangs in the air.

Around them, the mist thickened.
Far off, a bell rang sharp, metallic from the Ivory Hall.

Silas stood quickly. "That's my call. Training."

Nia rose too, brushing her robes. "Strategy drills?"

He nodded. "Something new.
Mother says we have to think three moves ahead now."

Nia's eyes narrowed. "Ahead of what?"

He didn't answer.

Just before turning, Silas hesitated.
He pulled something from his coat
a single white feather,
its edges too clean for nature,
too sharp to belong in mist.

"I found this near the Keep," he said.
"It felt… wrong to keep it."

Nia took it gently, tracing its delicate curve. "Thank you."

They parted without a wave. Without farewell.
That was their rule.

But as Nia tucked the feather into her satchel,
a tremor passed beneath her feet.
Small. But real.

Something had shifted.
A signal between squares.
A warning only some would feel.

The middle game had begun.

White Walls, Quiet War

The frost bit deeper around the edges of the Ivory Hall.
Wind hissed through tall, narrow windows,
rattling the glass like bones in a jar.
Fires burned low in the ornate hearths
more for form than warmth.

Cold here wasn't just temperature.
It was principle.
It kept things still.
Predictable.
Under control.

In the High Chamber,
where ceilings disappeared into black rafters,
the White King and Queen stood over the Strategy Table
a flawless marble replica of the Board.
Each square etched, numbered, and polished.

Sterile.
Lifeless.
Unlike the real game below.

King Alaric leaned on his cane, though he didn't need it.
It gave him an air of patience. Of deliberation.
His fingers hovered above the Black-side squares,
tracing invisible paths.

Queen Isolde stood opposite, arms folded,
her gaze fixed like frost.
"They're multiplying," she said.
"Their inventions. Their stories. Their alliances."

"Let them," Alaric murmured.
"It's noise."

"Noise becomes rhythm,"
came a quiet voice from the side.

Blanche, the White Rook, had stepped forward.

She rarely spoke unless summoned.
But tonight, the air in the chamber felt taut.

"And rhythm," she continued,
"builds momentum.
Momentum becomes movement.
And movement..."
She placed a pale stone on d5.
"...is what topples empires."

King Alaric nodded slowly.
"And movement," he said,
"makes them believe they don't need permission."

By the frosted glass,
Knight Gideon tapped the hilt of his blade.
"You mean to provoke them?"

"I mean to prepare," the King answered.
"We'll shift the boundaries.
A few new laws. Quiet restrictions.
Revisions masked as reforms.
Let them believe they've advanced."

Isolde's smile was glass.
"Let the Pawns think they've reached the eighth rank...
then redefine what that square means."

A ripple of amusement passed through the room.
Not laughter.
Approval.

Lucien, the White Bishop, lingered at the doorway.
Uninvited, as always.
Drawn by fire, but offering no warmth.
His voice cracked like cold parchment.
"And if they refuse to follow the new rules?"

Gideon spoke before Alaric could.

"Then they've left the game.
And pieces that leave the game…
can be cleared from the board."

No one met his eyes.

Blanche moved closer,
placing a second token on e4.
"We start here.
Trade.
Then education.
Then language."

"One square at a time," Isolde echoed.

"They won't notice," she added softly.
"Not at first.
And when they do…
the opening will be over.
And the middle game already lost."

Alaric gave a small nod.
"Begin the offering.
Let it look like a gift."

The fire snapped.
Another log cracked open like a bone.

And far below,
in the center of the Board,
where mist had only just begun to lift
something unseen shifted.

A faint tremor beneath the marble.
A disturbance in the air.
A memory,
pulling at the corners of the game.

A silent signal:
The Queen's side was no longer idle.

And not all Pawns followed rules.

A SPARK OF GENIUS

The sun rose slow and golden over Onyx Keep,
dripping light onto its towers like honey over stone.
The Board glowed where it touched the southern squares
a warmth not just of climate,
but of movement,
of mind,
of making.

Within those radiant walls,
the Black Family thrived.

Rook Kofi stood in the library tower,
sorting scrolls older than borders.
His lips moved in rhythm,
murmuring the names of Ancestors
not as ritual,
but as invocation.
Each name placed like a piece.
Each story, a strategy.

In the Maker's Courtyard below,
Pawns spun wheels,
fired kilns,
stitched banners,
brewed tinctures,
and bent the rules of design.

Nia barefoot, mud-streaked, and humming
shaped clay for a cooling jar system she swore
would keep herbs fresh past first frost.

"You're bending the neck wrong,"
called Knight Tariq from above.

"I'm bending it better," she shot back,
without looking up.

The Keep pulsed with this kind of defiant joy
not rebellion,
but rhythm.
Not resistance,

but revision.

They played the same game.
But with different rules.
Rules they made for themselves.

Bishop Sade led a midday gathering beneath whispering trees,
teaching chants in a tongue older than either Keep.
Light-language, they called it.
Every phrase shimmered with coded meanings,
layered like moves within moves.

As the Pawns repeated the chant,
the wind answered
as if the trees remembered.

Above them, in the stargazer's observatory,
Knight Luma charted constellations
beside a chessboard etched into marble.
She mapped stars and squares in tandem
studying both for shifts in pattern.

"What are we looking for?" asked her apprentice, Ayo.

"Signals," Luma replied.
"Disruptions in rhythm.
False openings.
Quiet traps.
Everything speaks," she said.
"The Board.
The stars.
Even silence."

Queen Zahara moved quietly through the dusk-lit halls,
trailing the scent of sage and roasted yam.
She paused often never to interrupt
only to witness.

In the courtyard,

a young Pawn recited an invention poem.
Another sketched a pulley system in chalk.
Others argued over pattern logic,
their laughter never far behind.

She smiled.
Not because the kingdom was at peace.
But because it was alive.
Their power wasn't in defense.
It was in *possibility*.

This was not just a Keep.
It was a sanctuary of creation.
A pulse of intellect.
A drumbeat of shared momentum.

And yet...

A wind had changed direction.

In Luma's observatory,
a comet veered from its expected path.

In the library,
a scroll cracked at its spine.

In the Maker's Courtyard,
Nia's jar, once perfect, cooled unevenly.

And in the Queen's corridor,
a single parchment arrived unsigned,
delivered without fanfare.

Zahara read it once.
Then again.

Her eyes narrowed.
Not with fear.
But with readiness.

She turned to the nearest guard.
"Call the council," she said softly.

"It's not our move yet.
But the next square has changed."

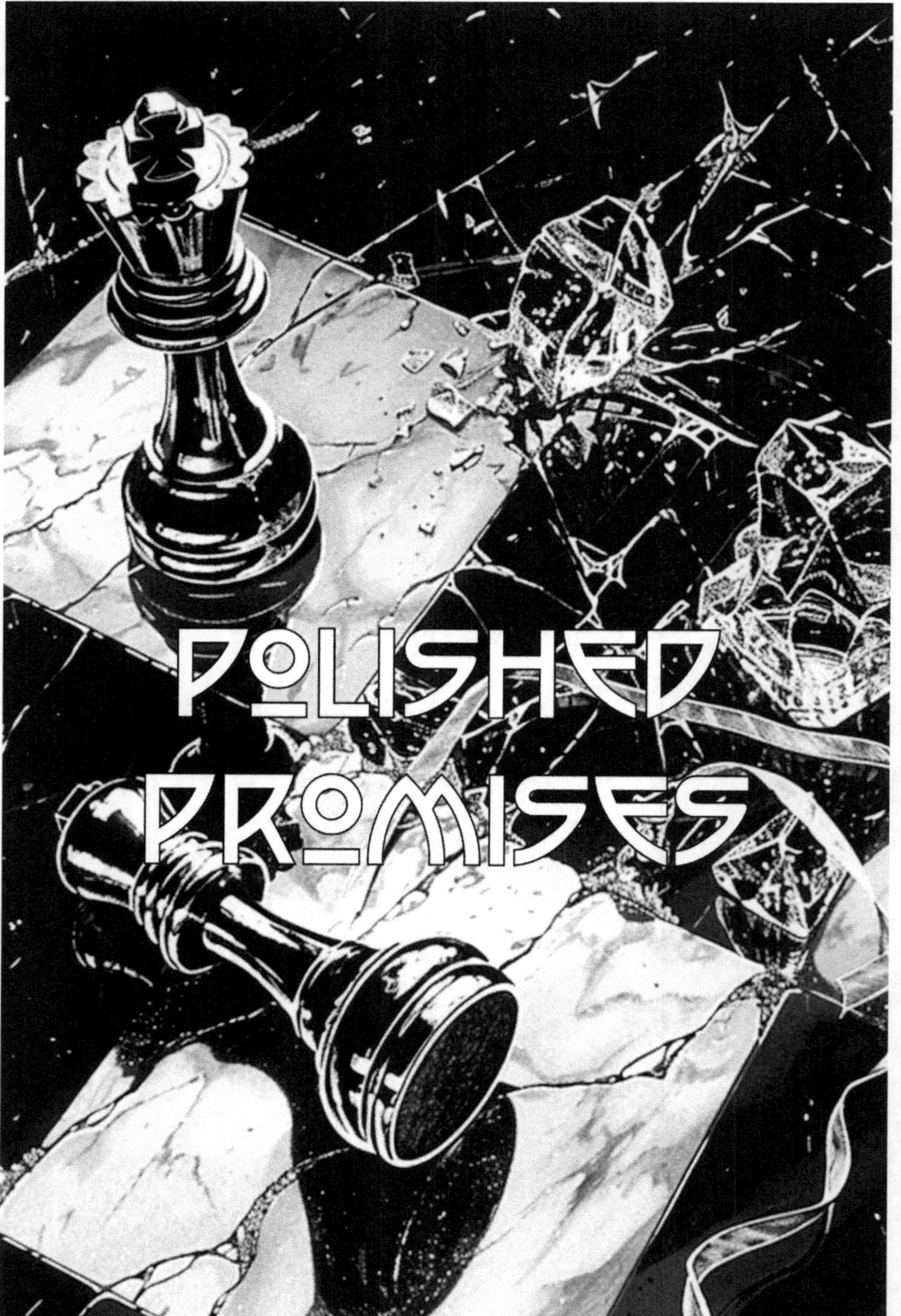

POLISHED
PROMISES

They came with silk and silver.

Crates stacked high with glinting tools,
scrolls written in unfamiliar tongues,
and ornaments carved for awe, not use
crystal figurines, glass flowers,
mirrored stars that cast no light of their own.

They called them gifts.

"The first of many,"
Knight Gideon declared, dismounting
with the grace of someone trained to appear humble.

Queen Isolde had called them
"offerings of goodwill."
King Alaric, more plainly,
had named it
"the beginning of shared prosperity."

Behind Gideon, the White Pawns moved in practiced silence.
Each bore something breakable
slender goblets wrapped in frostcloth,
a pale-framed mirror polished so fine
it reflected everything but truth,
and scrolls stitched with thread the color of moonbone.

They bowed often.
Smiled just enough.
And placed their gifts precisely.

In the Onyx Keep, the gifts were received with grace
if not belief.

Queen Zahara ran a hand over a folded cloth,
its shimmer like oil over water.
She smiled.
But said nothing.

"Why now?"
she asked softly, turning a silver compass in her palm.

The needle spun freely.
No direction. No pull.

King Jabari stood by the archway,
his eyes following the White Rooks
rebuilding the bridge that had not yet crumbled.

"They arrive with things," he murmured,
"we never lost."

The Black Pawns were curious.

Nia wrapped herself in the ivory-threaded cloth,
twirling beneath the lanterns.
"It glows," she whispered.
"Like captured sky."

Ayo tapped one of the glass carvings.
It rang like ice before breaking.

Tariq unrolled a scroll.
Lines. Columns. Numbers.
Rules. Not stories.
Accounting dressed as wisdom.

"This isn't knowledge," he said.
"It's measurement."

Still, the gifts were not rejected.

A feast was held.
Lanterns were lit.
Tables filled the courtyard with fruit and yam and fire-honey.

Drums beat in welcome,
but their rhythm was slower now
more cautious.

Knight Elara stood at the edge of the border,
hands behind her back,
eyes on the Keep she once entered only in secrecy.

She did not smile.

Far north, behind the marble doors of Ivory Hall,
Queen Isolde dipped her quill
into ink the color of silence.

She marked a symbol
a single square
beside a line of names etched in gold leaf.

"One Keep,"
she said to no one,
and drew a second mark beside the first.

Then she closed the book.

But did not put the quill down.

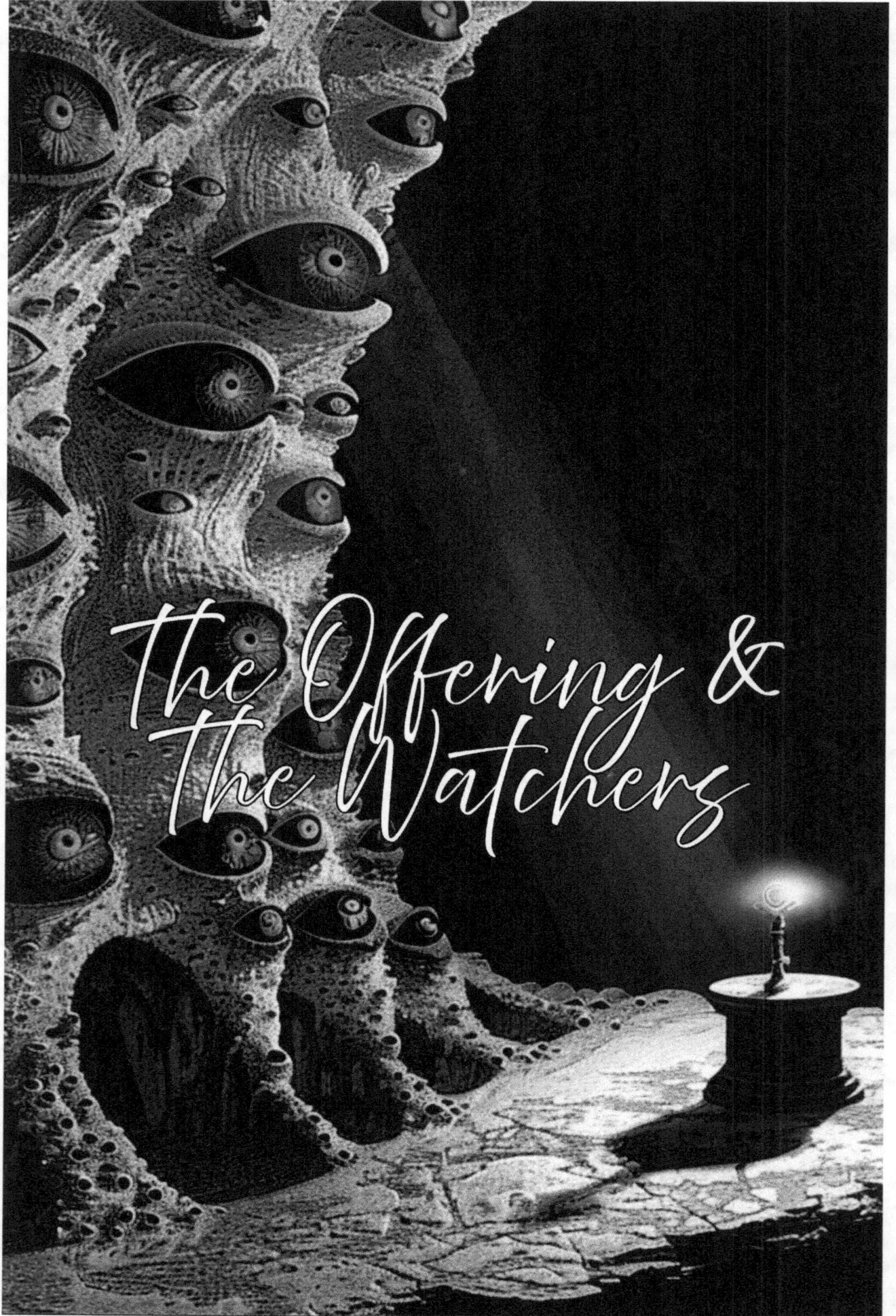

the Offering &
the Watchers

The sun poured low over the Onyx Keep,
dipping its light into the towers like ink into water.
Gold bled across the courtyards.
Heat softened the stone.
And all around, the rhythm of festival rose
drums, laughter, firelight.

It was the Night of Offering.
A tradition older than treaties.
Older, even, than the line across the Board.

Queen Zahara stood beneath the carved gate of stories,
her robes dyed from root and shadow,
her crown woven with brass and memory.

"Tonight," she said,
her voice woven into the drumbeat,
"we share what we have.
Not in trade, but in truth."

Around her, the Pawns of the Keep unveiled their gifts:
spice pouches stitched from pepperbark and saffron threads,
chimes made from southern sea-shells,
carved elephants etched with the names of ancestors,
light-wheels powered by steam and sun.

They were not gifts wrapped in apology.
They were artifacts of identity—
not concessions, but songs.

At the border rail,
where mist still shimmered from past trade storms,
Silas stood with a cherry-glass siphon in hand,
a present from Nia soaked in moon water and sweet defiance.
He did not cross the line.
But he held it in his hands like a question.

The White delegation arrived in sequence.
Alaric, in his high-collared ivory.
Isolde beside him, calculating silence.
Blanche, Cedric. Lucien. Benedict.

Their expressions carved from courtesy.

They bowed.
They nodded.
They accepted spice and light and warmth.
And offered nothing but thanks.

But their eyes moved too often
counting, not admiring.

As the feast bloomed in full color,
Gideon stood near a shadowed archway,
his gaze sweeping across the columns,
the courtyard's design,
the unseen flow of movement.

Blanche whispered beside him.

"See how their wealth shows itself.
It breeds belief in autonomy.
But belief can be redirected."

Gideon nodded.

"And every open hand teaches us the reach of their fingers."

Among the crowd,
Knight Luma handed out yam fritters
wrapped in golden leaf.
She caught a glimpse of Lucien and Benedict,
hushed in conversation
their attention not on the gifts,
but on the artisans.
The builders.
The patterns.

"Generosity is a mirror,"
Luma thought, turning away,
"It doesn't flatter.
It reflects."

Later, near the reflecting pool,
a lantern boat drifted softly past its edge.
Bishop Benedict excused himself,
drawing aside one of the Onyx Keepers.

"Where do you source the pepper bark?"
he asked, his voice casual.

But while the Keeper spoke,
Benedict's eyes never left
the carved map in the stone beneath them.
A trail of rivers,
a mark of valleys
and a vulnerable crossing point.

As the last lanterns dimmed
and the White family prepared to depart,
Isolde spoke without turning her head.

"We've woven presence," she said.
"Now we build reliance.
Next, we define direction."

Alaric watched the courtyard behind them.
Children still danced.
Fires still crackled.
The Onyx Keep hummed with joy.

"Leave them joy," he said.
"They'll cling to it.
And not notice what's missing later."

From the balcony,
Rook Kofi stood beside Zahara,
his voice low beneath the echo of retreating hoofbeats.

"They accepted the offerings," he said.
"But they measured."

Zahara closed her eyes.

"Then let the measure stand.

A gift is not a weakness.
But may it not become a debt."

Far away, in the frost-glass chambers of Ivory Hall,
the Watchers unfurled their scrolls.
They did not look at the gifts.
Only the geography.

One Keep marked.
One bridge rebuilt.
One celebration observed.
One silence recorded.

And in the margins of their maps,
they wrote nothing.

Just placed a single pale feather.

The First Gambit

Snow curled along the spires of Ivory Hall,
falling like whispered orders against the glass.
Inside, the Council Chamber gleamed
walls bone-white, table long and lacquered,
light catching on scroll edges and surgical instruments of thought.

Queen Isolde stood at its head,
draped not in furs, but in law.
Ink stained her fingers.
Cold ruled her voice.

"We begin today," she said.
"The Board favors precision."

Rook Blanche stepped forward,
her boots silent on the polished floor,
unrolling a new border map
etched in charcoal, not ink.
The Onyx Keep shimmered in the center,
surrounded by fine notations:
routes, rivers, rhythms to interrupt.

"We'll offer advanced tools," Blanche began,
"Soil enhancers. Irrigation spires.
Machines calibrated to needs they didn't know they had."

"Harvest guidance," Lucien added,
though his voice trailed like smoke.
"An education exchange, perhaps. Language assistance."

Knight Gideon arched an eyebrow.

"Wrapped in silk," he said.
"But what do we hide in the lining?"

Isolde's eyes glinted like frost catching candlelight.

"Rhythm," she replied.
"You don't win the game by overwhelming force.
You win by reshaping the tempo."

She dipped her quill into obsidian ink,
and drew a clean, assertive line
through the map's center

a new axis from which all movement might flow.

At the chamber's edge, a White Pawn entered.
Silas. Eyes down. Breath tight.
In his arms, a velvet box sealed with silver clasps.

Inside:
A timekeeper.
Gears of ivory.
Hands that spun in quiet synchrony
precise, unblinking, inevitable.

"For the Southern Royals," said Isolde,
"A gift. A gesture of timing.
So that all future moves... remain in step."

A moment passed.
Too long.
Even Lucien looked away.

Then, Isolde smiled gently.

"Send our finest.
Not the coldest faces
just the clearest ones."

Knight Elara, silent in the corner,
finally lifted her gaze.

"And when they open the gate?" she asked,
voice a thread in the still air.
"When they welcome us?"

Isolde folded the map like scripture.

"Then we offer refinement.
We help them master the game.
On our terms."

A slow breath moved through the council.
Not a cheer. Not applause.
Something quieter.

Surer.

Approval masked as peace.

Outside, the wind scraped frost from the tower roofs.
The same wind would reach the Onyx Keep by morning.
Carrying nothing but snow
and the faint ticking of strategy.

The gambit had begun.
Not with swords.
But with rhythm.
And rules rewritten.

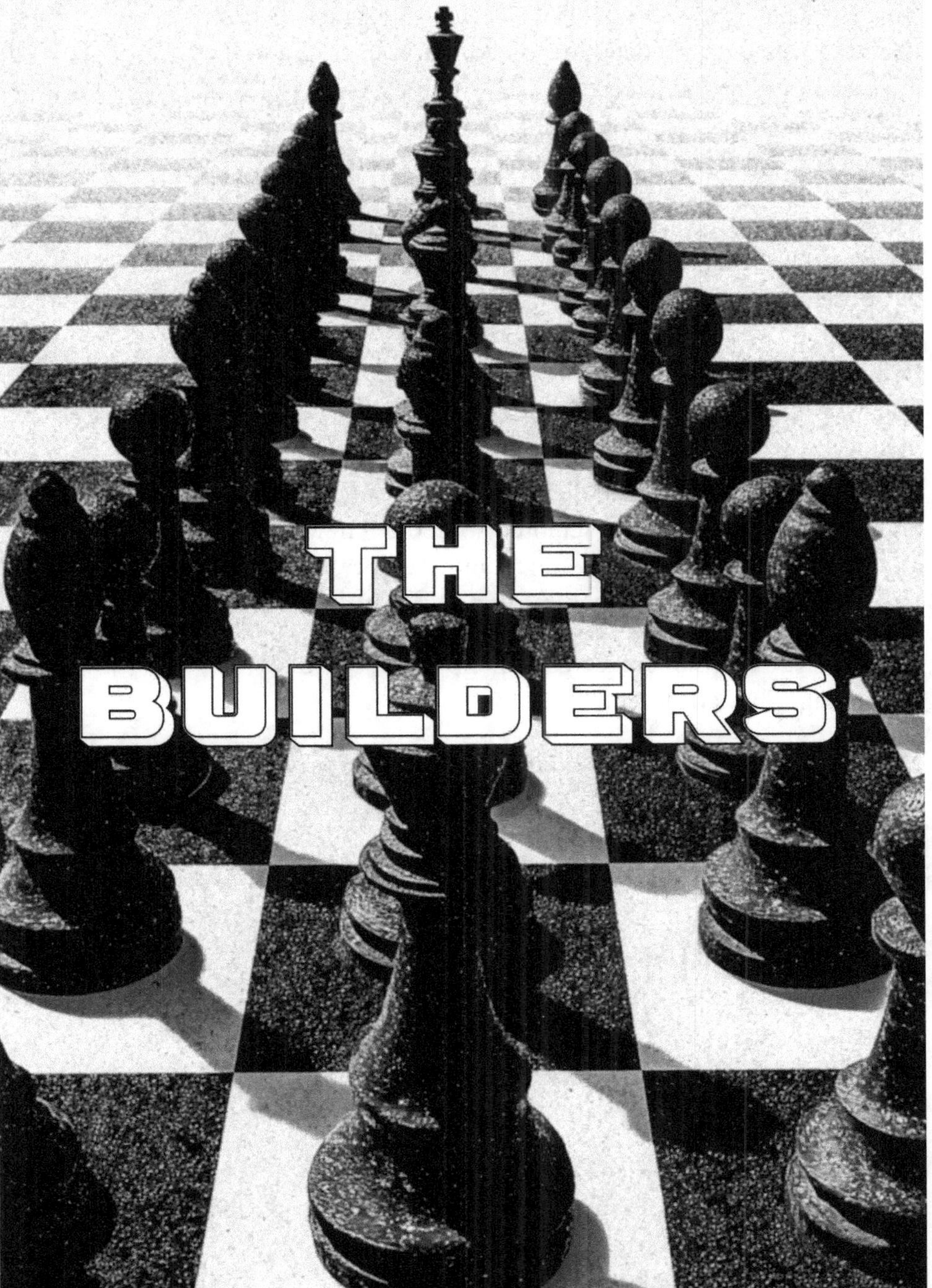
THE
BUILDERS

While the North drafted policies,
the South planted seeds.

In the Onyx Keep, no diagrams of conquest lined the walls.
No territories circled in red.
Instead: walls lined with blueprints drawn in charcoal dust,
garden terraces humming with new systems of thought.

Their minds moved forward
not toward power,
but possibility.

Knight Luma sprinted barefoot through the mist-paths,
a trail of scrolls tucked beneath one arm,
her fingers smudged with pollen and graphite.
She and Pawn Mensah had sculpted something new
an irrigation array tuned to sunlight and memory,
channels that sang open when morning hit just right.

"Not smart," Mensah corrected her, tapping a clay dial.
"Listening. That's different."

Luma laughed. "Then we've built ears into the ground."

Elsewhere, Bishop Sade taught history beneath a tapestry of shadow and
song.
No timelines. No tests.
Just rhythms:
the beat of migrations,
the cadence of names,
the pulse of resistance carried in lullabies.

She inked lessons onto rice leaves,
then folded them into floating lanterns.
When released into the dusk,
they became prayers and proof.

Queen Zahara's footsteps stitched the Keep together.

She walked without a guard,
pausing to listen in tool shops, kitchens, music rooms.

"What did you learn by accident today?"
she would ask.

And the answers
sometimes shy, sometimes sharp
became policy.

One apprentice had baked bread shaped like a broken river.
Zahara commissioned it for every Council meeting.

"So, we never forget what flow looks like."

On the western rooflines,
Cousin Ayo's solar vines now bloomed in thick coils,
coating towers in soft power.
"They're not plants," she said.
"They're stories that feed themselves."

In the dining halls, spice-maps changed daily
each dish built on an elder's memory of a harvest,
or a flavor once lost and found again.

And along the walkways,
small tiles etched by young Pawns
told the names of ancestors,
so no one's shadow vanished behind progress.

There were failures, too.

A staircase collapsed after a rush job.
Sade's lanterns once caught fire in a windstorm.
And two spice-maps ended in accidental chaos:
cinnamon with pickled yam.

But every flaw became material.

"The frost sends warnings," said Knight Tariq,
returning from the mountain line.

"But we don't build warnings.
We build warmth."

No one mentioned the gifts from Ivory Hall.
No one polished the compass
or used the silken ledgers.

They sat, untouched, in a side hall
too clean to be trusted.
Too quiet to be part of this rhythm.

The Keep did not look north.
It looked forward.

The Board stretched in every direction.
And here, where the sun moved without permission,
the Builders carved their answers into light.

LINES REDRAWN

Snow fell heavier now in Ivory Hall,
layering ambition in quiet folds of white.
Each flake a silence.
Each drift a cover.

In the War room, Queen Isolde stood before the towering map
a monument of pale marble carved to mimic the Board.
The Keep's positions gleamed beneath the glass;
but it was the new threads red, thin, taut that redrew the story.

They stretched across the middle territories,
threading through grain routes, school systems, and song hubs.
Each one marked a signature,
a smile,
a softened agreement.

"These lines," Isolde murmured,
"are not boundaries.
They are permissions."

Knight Gideon stood beside her; gloved hands folded.
He watched as a thread connected the Maker's Corridor
to a new Bureau of Trade Relations an office built in the name of "growth."

"They've disarmed their border Rooks," Gideon reported.
"Said it was a gesture of trust."

"Good," Isolde replied, eyes never leaving the map.
"Trust gives us reach."

Rook Blanche entered, snow trailing from her shoulders.
She nodded once.

"We've been invited to the Spring Games," she said.
"Hosted at center Keep.
Zahara signed it herself."

The Queen's smile returned, thin as the etching on a blade.

"Excellent. That gives us time."

Time to reshape language.

Time to scatter "optional reforms" into regional schools.
Time to publish new songbooks that taught children how to harmonize in one key only.

"They believe this is alliance," Gideon said again, almost carefully.

Isolde turned to him fully now.

"Exactly. That is the beauty of it.
They mistake hospitality for surrender."

Outside, frost scabbed over the courtyard walls.

Young White Pawns drilled beneath torchlight,
their boots striking in perfect rhythm,
their postures clean, absolute.
Every hand moved in sequence.
Every lesson, memorized.

Within the War room, the fire guttered once.
Someone closed a window, as if to keep something from escaping.

The Queen lifted her goblet silver, thin, gleaming like intention.

"To the long game," she said.
"To threads that look like bridges…
until they pull."

The Rooks drank.
The Bishop blessed the toast.

And across the map quiet, nearly hidden
one thread slid loose from its tack.
It curled near the southern edge.
Danced once in the warm air rising from Onyx Keep.
Then went still.

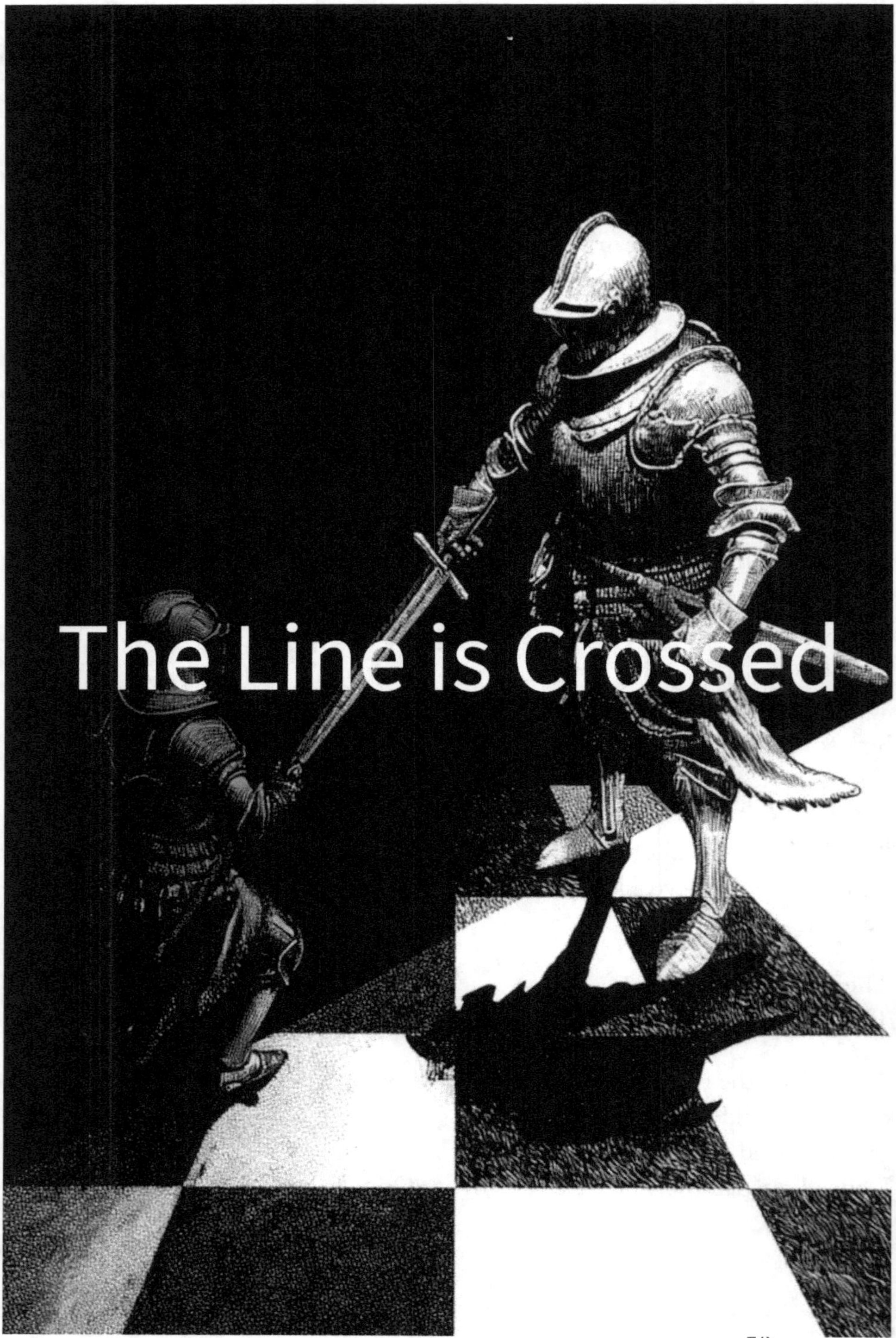

The Line is Crossed

It began with smoke.
Not warmth.
Not warning.
But something quieter.
Intentional.

Strange wisps curled up over the center squares
neither from the sunbaked stoves of Onyx Keep,
nor the frost-fed hearths of Ivory Hall.
It rose from a different fire.
A colder one.

Knight Tariq noticed it first.
He was patrolling the outer groves,
humming an old rhythm under his breath,
when his horse stiffened
ears twitching, muscles coiled.
Tariq lifted his head.

Burnt copper.
Damp parchment.
A scent that didn't belong.

He followed it
across the familiar paths,
past carved boundary stones,
and into the no-man's grove
where once
children had traded games, songs, carved lions and frozen flowers.

Now, a White Rook stood in the clearing,
driving stakes into thawed ground.
Above him, tall silver flags flared against the gray sky.
Beneath them, a structure new, unannounced
fastened into the soil like a blade.

Tariq's eyes narrowed.
This wasn't outreach.
This wasn't balance.

This was a move.

Back at Onyx Keep,
Queen Zahara received a scroll.
Polished parchment. Elegant script.

"An invitation to a celebration of shared progress,"
it read.
Signed by Queen Isolde.
Stamped with a new crest:
two hands clasped
across a single square.

Zahara's brow furrowed.

"We never approved this emblem," she murmured.

She didn't tear the scroll.
But she didn't smile either.

Rook Kofi was sent to observe.

At Ivory Hall's plaza,
he was greeted not with music,
but mimicry.

Black inventions stood beneath white glass
renamed, repainted, relabeled.

The memory-funnel Bishop Sade's students had carved?
Now painted pale and titled: *Inspired Mechanism: Joint Innovation.*

A childhood chant Nia had once taught in the orchard?
Now echoed in clean voices
stripped of its cadence,
twisted into choral symmetry.

No authors.
No origins.
Just silence where credit should be.

Kofi stepped back.
Not because he was afraid
but because he understood what this meant.

A celebration, yes.

But of erasure.

Back in Onyx Keep,
the wind changed.

Bishop Sade called the elders into council.
Knight Luma returned from patrol with her eyes hard as flint.
Even Nia noticed.
The kitchens were quieter.
Laughter dimmed.

Tariq stopped roaming.
Kofi stopped humming.
Ayo stopped sketching in the margins of her scrolls.

The rhythm still beat
but it was no longer smooth.

In Ivory Hall,
Queen Isolde stood before the War Map.

"Did they respond?" she asked.

Rook Blanche entered.

"No message. No envoy. No protest."

Isolde smiled, almost gently.

"Then they understand."

She turned from the Board.
Folded her hands.

"One Keep down."

And behind her, the center line on the map
quietly faded to white.

Checkmate

Snow fell on Onyx soil.
It did not belong.
It arrived like a hush before a scream
too soft, too soon, too cold.

At first, no one spoke of it.
The Keep had weathered stranger things.
But this was not weather.
It was omen.

On the high terrace,
King Jabari stood silent,
his gaze fixed on the northern sky.
Below, the children moved in slow formations
staffs spinning, feet grounded.
But the rhythm was off.
Even the drums hesitated.

Bishop Sade murmured incantations beneath her breath.
Not for ceremony.
But for warning.

Knight Tariq circled the outer walls,
not once, but three times before noon.
He saw no threat.
But still, the snow fell.

Then came the sound.
Bells.
Clear, melodic
the kind used to mark weddings, or victories.
But they rang out with no cause.
Only arrival.

White Rooks crossed the threshold.
Not armored.
Robed in lace and pale linen,
hands full of scrolls and sculpted symbols.

"We come in peace," they said,
placing gifts at the gates.

A music box.
A mirror.
A blade carved into a dove's shape.

Queen Zahara stood unmoving.
It was Jabari who nodded.

"We'll receive them," he said.

Inside the Grand Hall,
wine was poured.
Harmonies plucked softly.
Toasts were made to "shared futures,"
"bridges restored,"
and "the promise of unity."

But unity does not burst from disguise.

In one breath, the dancers turned.
In the next,
the weapons appeared.

From under their sleeves,
from hollowed scrolls,
from the hollow courtesies.

Chains uncoiled.
Smoke thickened.
And from beneath the performers' feet,
White Knights emerged
no longer cloaked.
Only prepared.

Knight Luma's warning cut the air:

"To the gates!"

But already, the Keep was splintering.
Staggering.

Bishop Sade raised her staff to shield the youngest.

Tariq reached for his blade
but was struck before he could unsheathe it.
The courtyard flooded with confusion,
not just of bodies,
but of betrayal.

And at the heart of it
King Jabari.

Not struck down.
Taken.
Silenced.
His arms bound by spell and rope.
Dragged from the hall
before Zahara could reach him.

She ran.
Too late.

Her scream cracked the rafters
the sound of heritage torn in half.

A white banner rose from the eastern tower.
Sharp. Uninvited.
Wrong.

Far away,
in the frost-lit chambers of Ivory Hall,
Queen Isolde closed her book.

"Checkmate,"
she said to no one.

The Grand Hall emptied.
The air grew still.
Pawns were lined up.
Rooks burned behind shuttered doors.
The soil of the Keep, once soft with music,
was packed hard with footprints not their own.

Zahara's crown lay in pieces on the stone steps.
Unclaimed.
Unbroken only in spirit.

And the snow?
It melted.
Fast.
Too fast.

Revealing the true shape beneath:

The Board
trembling.
As if it, too,
had not consented
to this move.

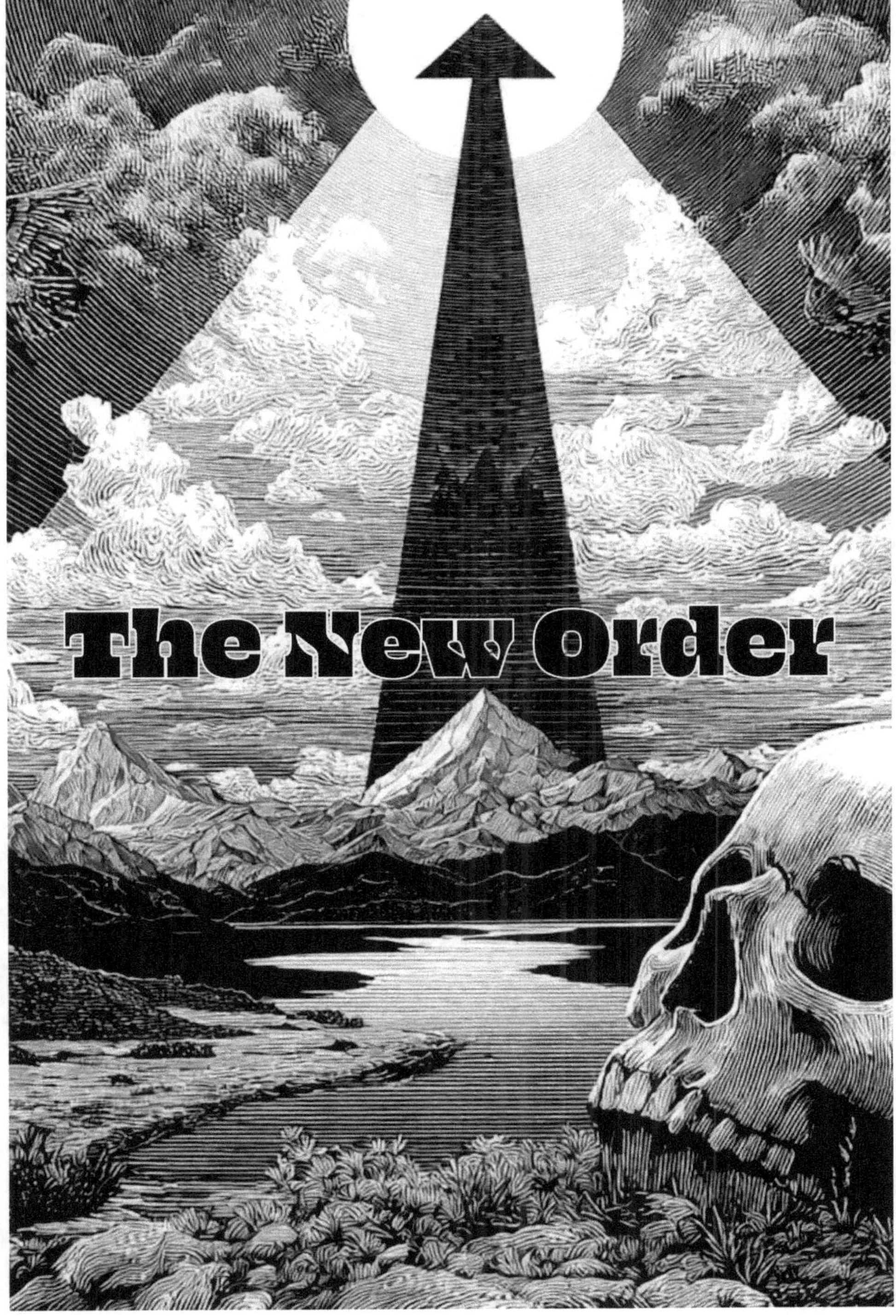
The New Order

The Board fell still.
But stillness is not peace.
It is silence.
Enforced.
Shaped into law.

In the years after the fall of the Onyx Keep,
a new narrative was scripted
not spoken by those who lived it,
but by those who claimed to have saved it.

"They welcomed our wisdom,"
the Ivory Hall declared.
"We brought structure."
"We restored order."
A lie repeated in polished halls
until even echo forgot the truth.

Scrolls were rewritten.
Maps redrawn.
History carved from bone and frost.

No statue stood for Zahara.
None for Jabari.
But alabaster likenesses of Queen Isolde multiplied
always open-handed, always above.
Beside her, King Alaric in sculpted serenity,
his crown lifted by others' labor.

Across the Board,
Black memory was unthreaded.

The Keep remained,
but its walls were washed pale.
Its corridors quieted.

Pawns no longer had names
only numbers.
Only tasks.

Knights were reassigned

not to protect,
but to police.

Bishops were forbidden to gather.
Forbidden to speak of stars,
or stories,
or self.

The great Rook libraries
stripped.
Books repurposed.
Scrolls whitewashed.
Memory, archived,
then sealed away.

Above the gate:
a single word etched in white stone:

Unity.
But the unity was brittle.
Unspoken rules multiplied.

The Ivory Hall moved without restriction.
Crossed lines without cost.
Spoke languages they'd once silenced.
Claimed symbols they'd never earned.

The game continued.
But no one believed it fair.

A Black Pawn who asked questions?
Dismissed.
A Black Knight who acted without permission?
Disciplined.
A Black Queen who dared to speak with fire?
Silenced.

They called it "balance."
They called it "tradition."
But it was conquest
in costume.

The youngest were taught to thank their keepers.
To rehearse obedience before understanding it.
To call silence respect,
and exile improvement.

Even the Board was silent.

One child, eyes wide, asked:

"Why do the windows not open?"

And the overseer replied:

"Air must be filtered for safety."

Another, while sweeping the empty archive halls, whispered:

"Who built these shelves?"

"Builders don't ask questions,"
came the reply.

Songs faded.
Rituals dimmed.
Names were erased from the walls.
But not from the stone.

Because deep beneath the Keep
beneath dust, beneath doctrine
something pulsed.

A thread of sound,
a flicker of rhythm.

Not yet music.
Not yet movement.

But close.
Very close.

The Board did not forget.
It remembered.
It waited.

Embers
Beneath the Stones

The first spark did not burn.
It **remembered**.
A single word,
scratched in chalk on a quiet square
gone by morning,
but not unnoticed.

A hum in the corridor,
a note older than laws,
caught and echoed
by a child too young to know
it was once forbidden.

The Onyx Keep, though painted pale,
still pulsed beneath the surface.
Not with rage.
With rhythm.

In the kitchens,
two Pawns kneaded dough by feel,
not measure.
Their hands moved with a tempo
their ancestors once clapped beneath stars.

In the courtyards,
a trio of Knights traced drills
from an old dance.
Not military steps,
but memory
coded in footfalls, passed in secret.

Ayo, now grown,
braided her hair with intention
each twist a syllable of story,
a lineage wrapped in silence.
She had been told to stop.
She did not.

Elsewhere, beneath the Keep,
an elder Rook with trembling fingers

etched symbols into the earth
patterns once used to map stars,
to teach history,
to pass time without losing truth.

At first, one child knelt beside him.
Then two.
Then twelve.

"What does it mean?" they asked.

"It means we were never lost,"
he whispered.
"Only buried.
Waiting."

Far across the Board,
in halls still lit by cold crystal and cleaner's oil,
the White Family remained
secure, settled,
reliant on old systems they no longer understood.

Queen Isolde had passed,
but her portrait stern and ageless still watched.
King Alaric's name still marked every law.
But time softened stone,
and silence no longer satisfied.

A young White Pawn,
curious and overlooked,
wandered the outer fields and found it
a **lion**, carved from driftwood,
curled beneath a frost-rooted tree.

Worn,
but whole.

He didn't know its maker.
Only that it didn't belong in snow.

He said nothing.
But he carried it with him.

Close.

Others, too, began to ask:
Why had they never heard certain songs?
Why were entire traditions labeled "disruption"?
Why were so many names left off the archives?

No answers came.
Only silence.
But silence no longer held.

And in the Keep's forgotten chamber
beneath veiled banners and boarded doors
a new gathering formed.
Small.
Deliberate.
Bright-eyed.

They studied the hidden maps.
They recited the names
carved beneath the walls of the Rooks.
They spoke in proverbs
the Elders had coded into lullabies.

And one night,
barely louder than the night wind,
a single Pawn asked:

"What if we moved first?"

Not to fight.
Not to seize.
But to **recall**.
To **reclaim**.
To **remind** the Board
what it was always meant to be.

The game shifted.
Barely.
A ripple beneath the marble.

A pause in the frost.
A whisper in the rhythm.

The embers glowed.
And beneath the square no one had claimed
not Black,
not White,
just *possibility*
a new move began.

The First Move

In the hush of dawn,
when frost still clung to the edges of the painted stone,
a Black Pawn knelt in the courtyard
no longer called Onyx.
But she knew better.

Her name was **Amara**.
Born beneath renamed towers.
Taught to walk in measured lines.
Taught to speak only what was allowed.

She had not seen the Keep in its full glory
but the stones had.
And today, they whispered.

Sweeping leaves from the corner square,
she uncovered not symmetry,
but story.
A carving nearly worn smooth
not a mark of conquest,
but of memory.
A language no longer taught.
A pattern no longer permitted.

She traced it slowly,
like prayer.

That night, she returned.
Not to protest.
Not to fight.
But to light a single flame
in a tower that no longer bore a name.

It had once been Bishop Sade's.
Though the stories had been scrubbed,
the stone still held breath.

The candle flickered
a signal only the Keep could read.

Across the corridors,

other Pawns stirred.

One tucked an old lullaby
into her apron pocket,
hummed it once,
then again.

Another pressed a slip of ink-stained cloth
into the wall crack where he'd once been punished
for asking who built the Board.

In the west wing,
a boy painted a board in charcoal
not neat, not perfect,
but alive.
His squares swayed, not straight,
but real.

They didn't call it protest.
They didn't need to.
They called it **remembering**.

And far away,
across cold lines etched in doctrine,
a White Pawn looked out his study window.

He had been taught rules.
He had memorized scripts.
But lately, the silence felt… wrong.

He opened a drawer
where a lion carved of driftwood waited,
smoothed by time,
carried by wonder.

He didn't know why,
but it mattered.

The Board did not tremble.
Not yet.

But beneath Amara's feet,
one square pulsed warm
as if something old had exhaled.

The first move was not loud.
It was not royal.
It was not even seen.

But it was made.
And the game would never be the same again.

The Pattern Reveals

The scrolls still sang their polished truths.
Order.
Gratitude.
The elegance of control.

But beneath the marble steps,
behind the stitched banners of unity,
something older moved.

Not in anger.
Not in haste.
But in rhythm.

Amara worked quietly.

She no longer copied the old symbols for memory alone
she did it for alignment.
Each curve, each stroke, etched not at random
but with intention.

Behind curtains.
Inside cracked wood panels.
Beneath the old benches
where no one looked,
she built a language
meant to be found.

One night, she scratched five shapes into a slat of forgotten floorboard.
When she returned the next day, a sixth had been added
not hers.

Another Pawn was watching.

They began to come,
one by one.

A girl with clay-stained hands brought a rusted compass
engraved with a script no teacher had explained.

A boy unrolled an old map

drawn in black stone ink
that showed the Keep not as a prison,
but as a pulse.

Another held up a broken pendant
a crown not bent in servitude,
but tipped in triumph.

Together,
they named nothing.
But they knew.

They met like shadows.
Spoke in echoes.
Moved like Knights
never straight, but always forward.

Far to the north,
the frost flinched.

Ivory Hall,
watching
but not understanding,
tightened its rules.

Pawns could no longer gather in fives.
Towers were renamed.
Old records "updated."
The Queen's crown on public murals
was reshaped flattened.

But the rhythm was too quiet to stop.
It had returned to breath.

In one forgotten corridor,
Amara knelt beneath a mural
scrubbed down to stone.

Her fingers found a trace
obsidian lines, rising from the dust.

A figure.
Not bowed.
Not broken.
A Queen, mid-step, eyes forward.

No caption.
No script.

But the shape said everything.

The Board, long silent,
inhaled.
Then exhaled.

Another square warmed.

The pattern was returning.

And the Keep was remembering itself.

The Movement

The wind changed.
Not with violence.
But with **intention**.

It didn't howl.
It hummed.

Low.
Layered.
A breath before the downbeat.

Then
it gathered.

Across the squares,
across the towers,
across memory itself,
a movement rose.

In the courtyard of the Onyx Keep,
young Pawns gathered
not as students, not as servants
but as strategists.

They wore no sigils.
No weapons.
They wore stories.

Etched into sashes.
Painted on palms.
Braided into hair.

They met beneath the walls
where old names had been scraped away
and **carved them back**.

They walked the garden paths
once trampled by invasion,
now reclaimed by rhythm.

There, beneath the faded statue of a girl

who once carved lions and gave them freely,
her story lived again.

"We were taught to move
one square at a time,"
said a young Pawn,
eyes bright with fire.
"But we've learned
that memory leaps.
That truth doesn't crawl.
It flies."

Others echoed her.
Some raised banners dyed in soil and flame.
Others drummed rhythms once banned.
One lit a small lamp for every lost name.

They did not call it rebellion.
They called it **returning**.

The Keep moved with them.

Rooks laid new foundations,
not for walls,
but for bridges.

Bishops no longer whispered.
They sang.
Verses stitched into air like spells of survival.

Knights arrived from long-forgotten borderlands.
Not hidden.
Not hesitant.
They returned as **guardians**.

And the towers opened
each one renamed for the erased.

Far to the North,
beneath frost-tinted windows,
the Ivory Hall listened.

Not all agreed.
But some had begun to wonder.

A Pawn named Crispin
unrolled scrolls he wasn't supposed to have.
He read them backwards.
Then upside down.
Until the lies unraveled.

"Who decides what's forbidden?" he asked.
No one answered.
So he kept asking.

He watched, from his narrow ledge,
as the Black Squares moved
not just in defiance,
but in design.

Each alliance forged,
each voice lifted,
made the Board **shift**.

What was once imbalance
was now momentum.

What was once silence
was now strategy.

The movement was not a wave.
It was a constellation.
Every spark connected.
Every piece, placed with purpose.

And for the first time
since the frost claimed the Keep
the pieces moved together.

Not for conquest.
Not for permission.

But because the Board was never meant
to belong to only one side.

It was meant
to move.

THE CRACKS IN THE BOARD

The first crack was quiet.
A thread-thin fracture along Square d4
a place once used to silence.
To punish.
To contain.

Now, it pulsed with footsteps and questions
too loud to erase.

Another crack appeared
beneath the west wing of the Ivory Hall,
where truth had been pressed thin
under centuries of polished lies.
Stone gave way
not to collapse
but to clarity.

And then came the tremors.

They moved beneath towers.
Beneath marble etched with false order.
Beneath the throne built on omission.

This wasn't destruction.
It was exposure.

The Board, once gleaming with symmetry,
began to show its seams.
Not from carelessness.
But from correction.

Beneath each polished square
were splinters
of stolen names,
of games played unfair,
of rules that had only ever served the few.

In the Onyx Keep, the people felt it.
Not with panic.

With **recognition**.

"The Board was never even,"
murmured an Elder Rook,
tracing a crack with reverent fingers.
"It only looked balanced
because we were forced to kneel."

Now
no one kneeled.

Pawns stood in formation,
not waiting to be moved,
but choosing their own steps.

Bishops preached openly
from towers rebuilt with purpose,
their sermons not about victory,
but vision.

Queens reemerged,
not just in murals,
but in memory
in method
in motion.

And the cracks?
They didn't break the Keep.
They **revealed it**.

Roots rose.
Light entered.
Drumbeats shook the stone.
Truth grew where silence had ruled.

Even in the far chambers of Ivory Hall,
some heard it.

Young Pawns paused mid-lesson
as vibrations hummed through the floor.

A White Bishop, once silenced for questioning,
unrolled an old scroll and whispered,
"We were wrong."

Others, younger
raised on conquest, not questions
stood frozen.

They had not written the rules.
But they had lived by them.
Benefited from them.
And now…
the Board was no longer theirs to dictate.

Outside the walls,
the lines between sides blurred.
Not from invasion.
From **memory**.

From names remembered.
From stories returned.
From movements too precise to stop.

This was not the end of the game.
It was its **unmasking**.

No longer rigid.
No longer rigged.

But remade.

Into something older than conquest.
Wiser than rulebooks.
And far more powerful
than any Crown had prepared for:

A match no longer theirs to control.

The Rewriting

The ink dried slowly
not on decrees
but on declarations.

Not written by the crowned,
but by the callused.

Scrolls unrolled across the Keep
not from above,
but from within.

Their authors were many:
young and old,
quiet and bold,
each hand steady,
each truth deliberate.

One scroll read:
**"The Queen did not fall.
She was buried
then reborn
in every act of resistance."**

Another:
**"A King who listens
can never be captured."**

The Onyx Keep breathed again.
Not with smoke,
but with stories.

Artists peeled whitewash from murals
not with blades,
but with fingers and fire.

Layer by layer,
the past re-emerged.

In the courtyards,
children played the old stories

not tales of conquest,
but of cunning, compassion, resilience.

They named each other
after legends never carved in stone.

"I'm Zahara today,"
one girl shouted,
leaping from square to square.
"You be Luma!"

And the game they played
wasn't about winning.
It was about remembering.

Across the Board,
the Ivory Hall shifted.

Silence, once sacred,
shuddered beneath the weight of questions.

A White Pawn named Callum
whispered to his tutor,
"Why were the Black pieces
always called wild?"

No answer came
but the question didn't vanish.
It *echoed.*

In the Hall of Records,
a long-sealed archive creaked open.

The Writings of Lucien
once locked in dust and disapproval
now lay in the open.

Letters.
Meditations.
Questions.
From a man who had once

dared to wonder aloud.

And slowly
truth began to unfasten the lie.

The new Kings
from both sides of the Board
spoke less.
Listened more.

They studied the old moves
not to reenact,
but to ask:
Why were they made?
And who did they serve?

The Rooks rebuilt
not fortresses,
but bridges.

The Bishops recovered
not dogma,
but dialect.

The Knights patrolled
not with weapons,
but with stories.

And the Queens?
They never stopped moving.

They led from the margins,
from dusk-lit drumlines
and memory-stitched banners.

From kitchen corners
where whispers carried strategy
like sacred thread.

The Board was no longer a battlefield.

It had become
a library.
A garden.
A song.

And though some still clutched
the old rulebook
they now played a game
they no longer understood.

A game
that no longer bent to them.

Checkmate
was no longer conquest.

It was chorus.
Reckoning.
Return.

And across every square
from the frostbitten North
to the sun-kissed South
the pieces moved.

Still deliberate.
Still dreaming.
But now
they moved together.

Final Move

The air was still.

The Board, once cracked and scorched by centuries of silence and strategy,
now pulsed with something older
a rhythm buried deep,
but never broken.

Across the southern squares,
the Onyx Keep stood once more.
Not hidden.
Not hushed.
Not bowed.

Its walls rose not from blueprints,
but from memory
from chants passed down through Pawns,
from carvings in corners once forbidden,
from lullabies hummed by Queens
whose names had been erased from scrolls
but not from blood.

The Keep had returned.

And with it
the Black Family.
Not as survivors.
As architects.

This time,
they were not alone.

From the frost lit North,
some had crossed the threshold
not to conquer,
but to listen.

Not all had forgotten.
Not all had remained blind.

And on the central square
once a stage for false treaties,

for stolen applause
stood something new.

A formation not built by power,
but by memory.

Queen Zahara's legacy
was no longer an echo.
It walked the Board
in the bodies of those
who had reached the edge
and rewritten the game.

Knights rode not for war,
but for truth.

Rooks carried blueprints
not for towers,
but for archives.

Bishops sang
in every tongue that had once been outlawed.

And the King
he did not command.
He listened.
Because he knew:
power lives
in every piece.

Once,
a storm had swept the Board.
Now came a stillness.

Not silence.
Calm.

Not surrender.
Arrival.

Then came the final move.

It was not loud.
It needed no fanfare.
No flags.

A Pawn
young, steady
stepped into the center.

Her crown was not granted.
It was grown
from names remembered,
from truths recovered,
from each step taken
against the grain of forgetting.

And when she stood
fully formed,
radiant,
uncaged
she looked to what remained
of the old regime and spoke:

"Checkmate."

It was not revenge.
Not a reversal.
It was return.

The game,
once twisted,
had been untwisted.

The rules,
once hidden,
had been reclaimed.

The Board,
once divided,
had been redrawn
not in conquest,
but in truth.

And as the sun rose
over ivory halls
and onyx walls alike,

a new rhythm
beat through the squares.

Not perfect.
Not final.

But right.

And this time
it would not be forgotten.
Not ever again.

About the Author

Nia Kweli is a writer, educator, and creative visionary passionate about guiding young readers to explore truth, history, and justice through bold, thought-provoking storytelling.
Check is her debut allegorical work an intricate story layered with symbolism, legacy, and the power of voice.

When she's not writing, Nia develops creative resources for students and educators through **Truth Busters**, a platform dedicated to critical thinking, meaningful conversation, and community engagement.

Learn more at www.truthbusters.info

▦ Keep the Conversation Going

Want to go beyond the story?

Scan the QR code below to visit the
Truth Busters landing page, where you'll find:

- ☐ Printable **worksheets and discussion prompts.**

- ☐ **Creative activities** inspired by *Check.*

- ☐ Tools to help young readers think critically and ask bold questions.

Download. Explore. Share.

Or visit:
www.truthbusters.info scroll to the bottom of the 'Beyond Truth Busters' page.

9 798994 200308